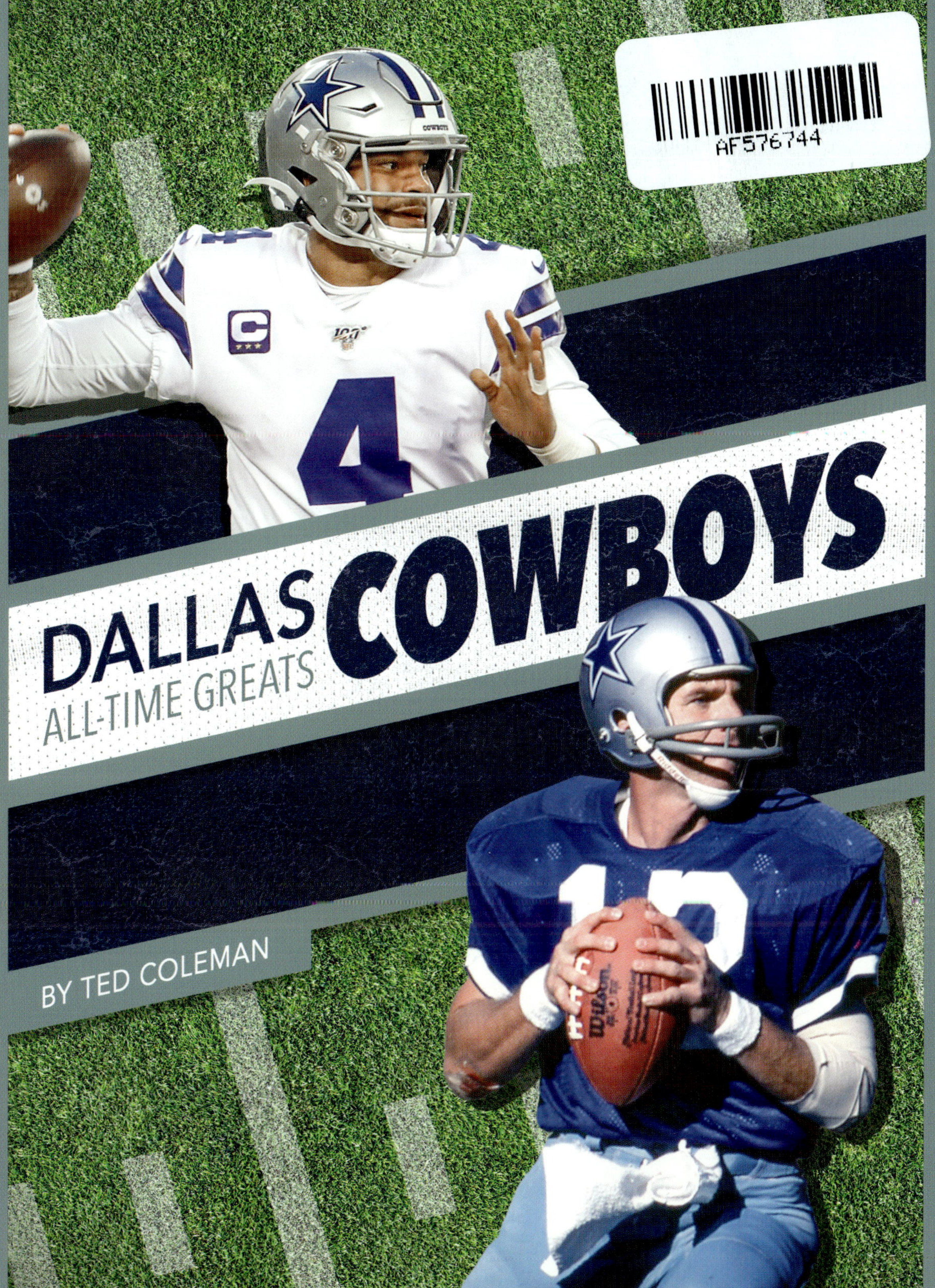

DALLAS COWBOYS

ALL-TIME GREATS

BY TED COLEMAN

Book design by Jake Slavik
Cover design by Jake Slavik

Photographs ©: Chris Szagola/AP Images, cover (top), 1 (top); Tony Tomsic/AP Images, cover (bottom), 1 (bottom); Al Messerschmidt/AP Images, 4; Peter Read Miller/AP Images, 7, 10; David Durochik/AP Images, 8; Doug Jennings/AP Images, 9; Linda Kaye/AP Images, 12; Paul Spinelli/AP Images, 15; Greg Trott/AP Images, 16, 21; Kirby Lee/AP Images, 18

Press Box Books, an imprint of Press Room Editions.

ISBN
978-1-63494-354-3 (library bound)
978-1-63494-371-0 (paperback)
978-1-63494-404-5 (epub)
978-1-63494-388-8 (hosted ebook)

Library of Congress Control Number: 2020952462

Distributed by North Star Editions, Inc.
2297 Waters Drive
Mendota Heights, MN 55120
www.northstareditions.com

Printed in the United States of America
082021

ABOUT THE AUTHOR

Ted Coleman is a sportswriter who lives in Louisville, Kentucky, with his trusty Affenpinscher, Chloe.

TABLE OF CONTENTS

LILLY
74

CHAPTER 1 COWBOYS LEGENDS

The Dallas Cowboys were not always a Super Bowl dynasty. In their first season of 1960, they didn't win a single game. They were one of the worst teams in the National Football League (NFL) in those early years. But they did have stars such as defensive tackle **Bob Lilly**. Lilly was nearly unstoppable. He made the Pro Bowl 11 times in his 14 seasons.

Lilly and cornerback **Mel Renfro** led the Cowboys' "Doomsday Defense." Renfro intercepted 52 passes during his career. That was the most in Cowboys history. The Doomsday Defense led the Cowboys all the way to a Super Bowl title in the 1971 season.

The Cowboys could also score. Receiver **Bob Hayes** was called "Bullet Bob" because of his unmatched speed. Hayes had been an Olympic-gold-medal sprinter. It turned out he could catch, too. Hayes led the NFL in receiving touchdowns twice.

Hayes received some of those passes from quarterback **Roger Staubach**. After serving in the US Navy, Staubach played 11 seasons with the Cowboys. He was known for his scrambling ability and for keeping plays alive. It didn't hurt

TOM LANDRY

Coach **Tom Landry** was known for two things. First, he always wore a fedora hat on the sidelines. Second, he won a whole lot of football games. Landry coached Dallas from 1960 to 1988. The Cowboys posted a winning record every year from 1966 to 1985. Landry also helped the team win two Super Bowl titles.

that offensive tackle **Rayfield Wright** was blocking for Staubach. Wright dominated the line. Staubach called him the best blocker in the game.

The Doomsday Defense received new life in the 1970s. Safeties **Cliff Harris** and **Charlie Waters** combined for 70 career interceptions. Harris played the position aggressively. In contrast, Waters studied the field, watching the quarterback's every move. Together, they shut down opposing offenses.

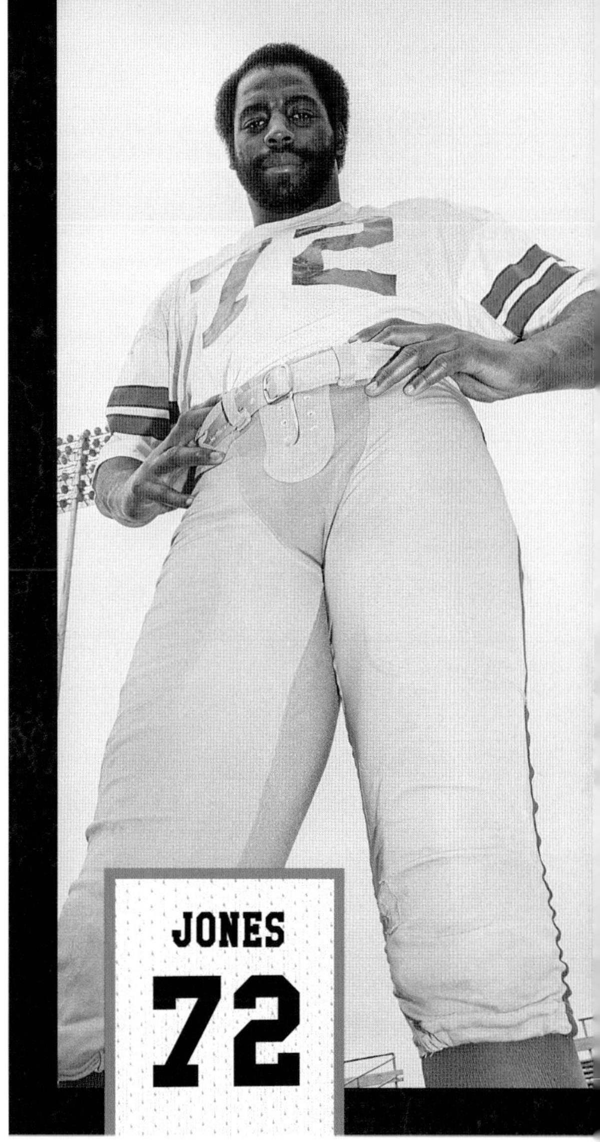

The Cowboys' defensive ends were **Harvey Martin** and **Ed "Too Tall" Jones**. At 6-foot-5, Martin was pretty tall himself. But at 6-foot-9, Jones towered over opponents. Both players were physical pass rushers. Alongside "Too Tall" Jones, Martin needed a nickname of his own. Fittingly, his became "Too Mean."

DORSETT
33

Randy White played the other key role on the Doomsday Defense. White lined up as both linebacker and defensive tackle during his career. He was quick, physical, and tough. In 14 seasons, he missed just one game. White and the Cowboys defense led Dallas to another Super Bowl title during the 1977 season.

Running back **Tony Dorsett** was named Rookie of the Year in 1977. He ran for 1,007 yards and 12 touchdowns that season. In his Cowboys career, he rushed for more than 12,000 yards. But another player soon came along to challenge that lofty mark.

STAT SPOTLIGHT

LONGEST TOUCHDOWN RUN

NFL RECORD

Tony Dorsett: 99 yards (1982)

AIKMAN
8
IRVIN
88
SMITH
22

CHAPTER 2
THE TRIPLETS AND MORE

After several losing seasons in the late 1980s, the Cowboys bounced back in the early 1990s. Many fans thanked "the Triplets." Receiver **Michael Irvin**, quarterback **Troy Aikman**, and running back **Emmitt Smith** led the Cowboys back to Super Bowl glory. Irvin came first in 1988. He used his size and strength to break away from defenders.

Aikman was next in 1989. He was known for his accuracy. He completed 61.5 percent of his passes. Aikman also won 90 games in the 1990s. No other quarterback won more.

Smith rounded out the Triplets in 1990. Starting in 1991, Smith topped 1,000 yards for 11 straight seasons. He shattered Tony Dorsett's team record for rushing yards. In fact, all the Triplets set team yardage records at their positions. But Smith took it to the next level by setting the NFL record for rushing.

Guard **Larry Allen** was a big reason Smith racked up all those rushing yards. Allen used his massive size and strength to open holes for Smith. In addition, Allen made 10 Pro Bowls as a Cowboy. That's more than any offensive player made in Cowboys history.

STAT SPOTLIGHT

CAREER RUSHING YARDS

COWBOYS TEAM RECORD

Emmitt Smith: 17,162

ALLEN
73

SANDERS
21

The Cowboys didn't win just with their offense. Defensive end **Charles Haley** played in Dallas from 1992 to 1996. During that time, he helped the team win three Super Bowls.

Deion Sanders was known as "Prime Time" because he always showed up in the biggest moments. Sanders excelled as a cornerback. He was also an electric returner. Sanders averaged 13.3 yards per punt return as a Cowboy. And he returned four punts for touchdowns. These exciting players helped make the Cowboys one of the best teams of the 1990s.

JOHNSON TO SWITZER

Head coach **Jimmy Johnson** led the Cowboys to two straight Super Bowl titles in 1992 and 1993. But a personal feud developed between him and the Cowboys' owner. Johnson left the team after the second title. **Barry Switzer** stepped in, and Dallas barely missed a beat. The team won another title in 1995.

ROMO
9

CHAPTER 3

NEXT TO WEAR THE STAR

After Troy Aikman retired in 2001, the Cowboys didn't have to wait long for their next franchise quarterback. He came from an unlikely place. No team even drafted **Tony Romo** in 2003. The Cowboys signed him later as a free agent. He went on to become the team's all-time leading passer.

STAT SPOTLIGHT

CAREER PASSING YARDS

COWBOYS TEAM RECORD

Tony Romo: 34,183

Romo had some help from **Jason Witten**. The star tight end didn't have great speed, but he could block as well as catch. By the time Witten retired, he was the team's all-time leader in receiving yards.

Sack machine **DeMarcus Ware** helped the Cowboys become a top-10 defense in 2007. Dallas went 13–3 that season. That was their most wins since 1992. But the Cowboys never reached a Super Bowl during the Romo era.

The Cowboys won 13 games again in 2016. That was the rookie season of

JASON GARRETT

Cowboys fans knew about **Jason Garrett** long before he became head coach in 2010. Garrett was a backup quarterback for the Cowboys in the 1990s. He famously led Dallas to a win over rival Washington on Thanksgiving Day in 1994. As coach, Garrett was second only to Tom Landry in career wins.

running back **Ezekiel "Zeke" Elliott**. Zeke racked up more than 6,000 yards in his first five seasons.

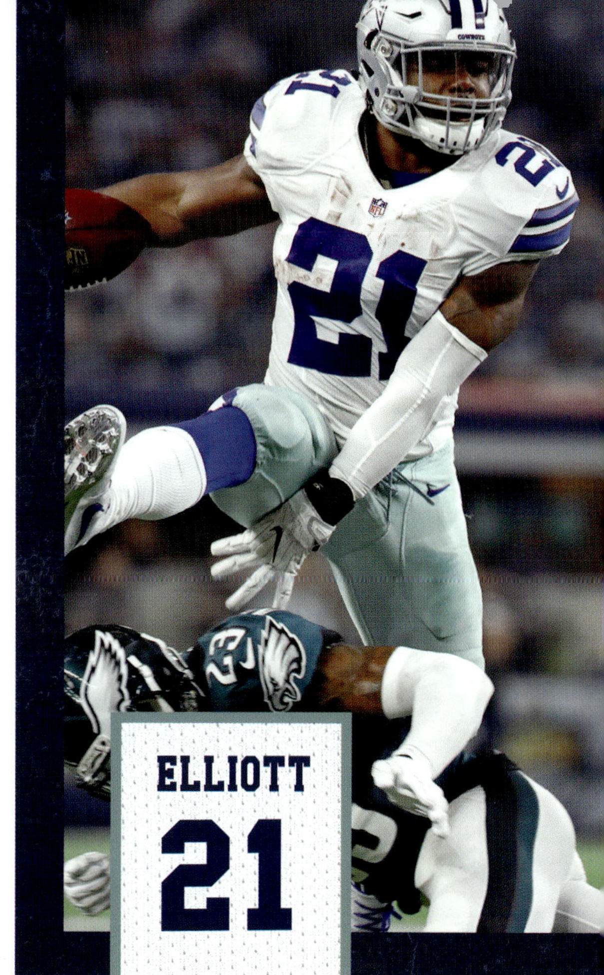

Dak Prescott became the next Cowboys franchise quarterback in 2016. Prescott was just as good at running as he was at passing. His dual-threat play made him tough to match up against. Fans hoped players such as Prescott and Elliott would lead the Cowboys into their next Super Bowl era.

TIMELINE

1960
1970
1980
1990
2000
2010
2020
MEL RENFRO
(1964–77)
RAYFIELD WRIGHT
(1967–79)
CLIFF HARRIS
(1970–79)
HARVEY MARTIN
(1973–83)
RANDY WHITE
(1975–88)
MICHAEL IRVIN
(1988–99)
EMMITT SMITH
(1990–2002)
LARRY ALLEN
(1994–2005)
TONY ROMO
(2003–16)
DEMARCUS WARE
(2005–13)
DAK PRESCOTT
(2016–)
BOB LILLY
(1961–74)
BOB HAYES
(1965–74)
ROGER STAUBACH
(1969–79)
CHARLIE WATERS
(1970–81)
ED JONES
(1974–78, 1980–89)
TONY DORSETT
(1977–87)
TROY AIKMAN
(1989–2000)
CHARLES HALEY
(1992–96)
DEION SANDERS
(1995–99)
JASON WITTEN
(2003–17, 2019)
EZEKIEL ELLIOTT
(2016–)

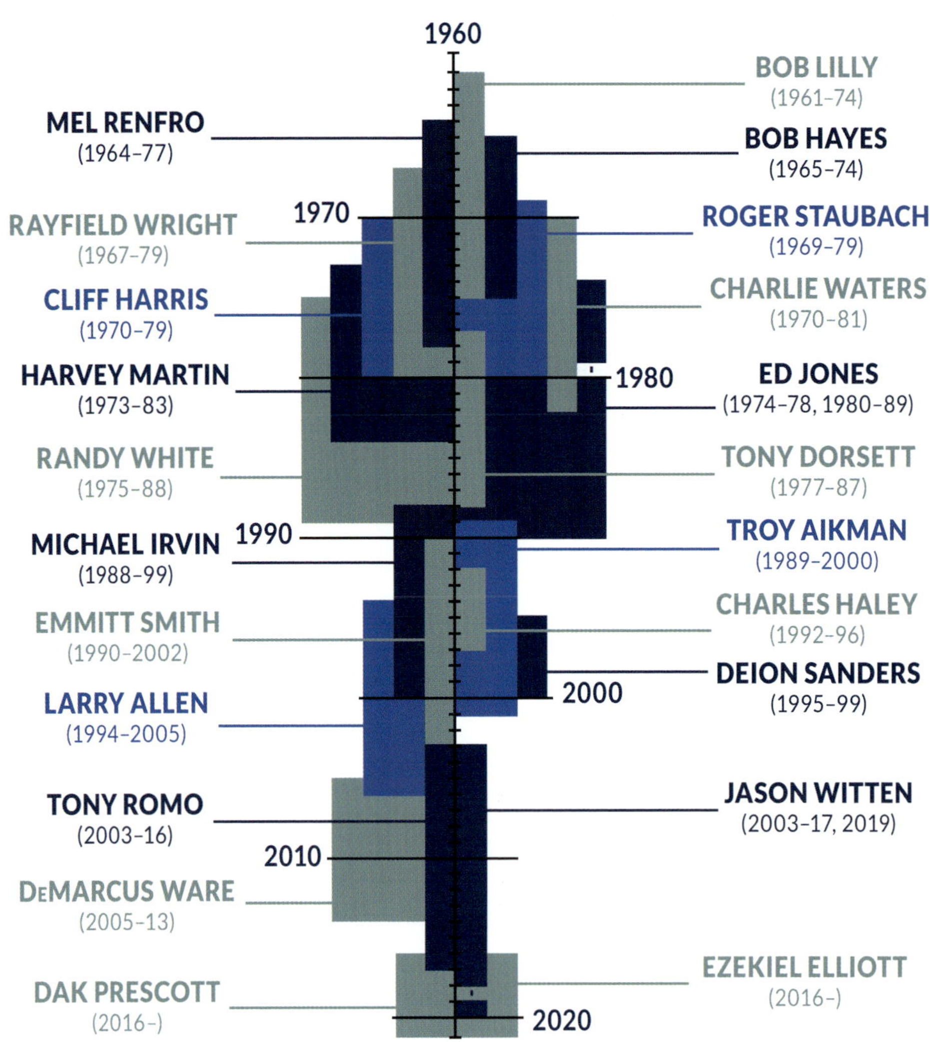

TEAM FACTS

DALLAS COWBOYS

Founded: 1960

Super Bowl titles: 5 (1971, 1977, 1992, 1993, 1995)*

Key coaches:

Tom Landry (1960–88), 250–162–6, 2 Super Bowl titles

Jimmy Johnson (1989–93), 44–36–0, 2 Super Bowl titles

Barry Switzer (1994–98), 40–24–0, 1 Super Bowl title

Jason Garrett (2010–2019), 85–67–0

MORE INFORMATION

To learn more about the Dallas Cowboys, go to **pressboxbooks.com/AllAccess**.

These links are routinely monitored and updated to provide the most current information available.

**1966 through 2020*

GLOSSARY

cornerback
A defensive player who covers wide receivers near the sidelines.

dynasty
A team that has an extended period of success, usually winning multiple championships in the process.

franchise quarterback
A quarterback capable of leading a team for a number of years.

free agent
A player who can sign with any team.

linebacker
A player who lines up behind the defensive linemen and in front of the defensive backs.

Pro Bowl
The NFL's all-star game, in which the league's best players compete.

rookie
A professional athlete in his or her first year of competition.

sack
A tackle of the quarterback behind the line of scrimmage.

INDEX